# The MASKED MAVERICK

by Jacqueline K. Ogburn

pictures by Nancy Carlson

**LOTHROP, LEE & SHEPARD BOOKS**

**NEW YORK**

For Claire Carson Deahl
—J.K.O.


For Robbie Little,
thanks for your help
—N.C.

First Edition  1  2  3  4  5  6  7  8  9  10

Library of Congress Cataloging in Publication Data
Ogburn, Jacqueline K. The Masked Maverick / Jacqueline K. Ogburn ;
illustrated by Nancy Carlson.
p.    cm.    Summary: The Masked Maverick, the toughest wrestler in his league, tries
to gain popularity with the booing crowd by revealing the sweetness of his true nature.
ISBN 0-688-11049-5. — ISBN 0-688-11050-9 (lib. bdg.)  [1. Wrestling—Fiction.]
I. Carlson, Nancy L., ill.  II. Title.  PZ7.O3317Mas  1994  [E]—dc20  92-1669  CIP  AC

The Masked Maverick was the best wrestler in the American Wrestling League.

When he threw his opponent to the mat at the end of an airplane spin, the tremors were felt all the way back to the twenty-third row. When he gave his Maverick Victory Yodel, people in the first three rows had to cover their ears.

**TRAINING**

monday- hamburger
        fries - 2 sit-ups

Tue. EAT LOTS - RUN
     one block.

wed. EAT A chuck-
     Roost. / Rest.

Thurs. lift weights
Then eat fries, and
MALT.

FRIDAY- Meat loaf

GREETINGS

But even better than his moves in the ring was the Masked Maverick's costume: knee-high flame-red wrestling boots, black trunks, a red-lined black cape, and best of all, a marvelous black mask. His whole head was covered in black, and red flames circled his eyes and mouth. The Masked Maverick had designed it himself and had made his first mask out of soft black leather and red silk. He now had seven copies, one for every day of the week. No one in the wrestling world had ever seen the Masked Maverick's face—not the other wrestlers, not the fans, not even his manager.

The Masked Maverick loved his work. He had only one problem. The crowd didn't love him.

Whenever the referee held up his arm as the winner, they booed. BOOOO! Whenever he gave his Maverick Victory Yodel, they hissed. HSSSSS! And whenever he strapped on the championship belt, they did both. BOOOO! HSSSS! BOOOOOOO!

It was very depressing.

When he won the Intercontinental Fall Frenzy Free-for-All, he was booed all the way out of the arena. The Masked Maverick was fed up. In his private dressing room, he told his manager, "I can't stand being booed and hissed anymore. I'm going to quit."

"You can't quit," said his manager. "You're the best wrestler in the whole league. The crowds boo because you're so tough in the ring. If they knew what a sweetheart you really are, they would love you as much as I do. I have an idea that will show them. Trust me."

The Maverick's next fight was with Hammerhand Hannibal.
Hammerhand was a great, burly fellow with long, curly hair and
a huge handlebar moustache, but no mask. He paraded into the
arena, swinging two fifty-pound sledgehammers, clanging them
over his head and behind his back.

The Masked Maverick marched to the ring carrying a huge
bouquet of flame-red poppies. He threw some flowers at the
crowd and they laughed. Well, he thought, laughing is better than
hissing. He gave a poppy to Hammerhand after they shook hands
and presented the rest to the ring announcer.

While Hammerhand was gaping at his flower, the bell rang. The Maverick took him down with a flying drop kick. Hammerhand staggered to his feet. The Masked Maverick swung him around

and around and into the ropes. Hammerhand bounced back,
and the Maverick dropped him with a clothesline to the
throat. Hammerhand Hannibal was down for the count.

The referee raised the Maverick's hand high over his head. The Masked Maverick waited for the applause. But all he heard were boos and hisses and even a few Bronx cheers. The poppies had not done the trick. The Masked Maverick sighed.

In his dressing room, his manager said, "Don't worry, M.M., I've got another idea."

That Sunday, the Masked Maverick was up against Mad Dog Markowitz. Mad Dog had been the league champion before the Maverick won the title from him, so this was a grudge match. The tickets sold out so fast that not even Mad Dog's grandmother could get a seat.

Straining the end of a twenty-foot chain held by his trainer, Mad
Dog Markowitz charged into the arena. Mad Dog had a thick,
studded dog collar around his neck and a giant, greasy ham bone
in his fist—but no mask. His Mad Dog Moon Howl was almost as
good as the Maverick Victory Yodel, but only the fans in the first
row had to cover their ears.

The Masked Maverick stepped into the spotlight on the ramp.
The crowd snickered. The champ was wearing a new costume: a
white cape with a pink lining, pink boots, and white tights covered
with pink and red hearts. Tonight his mask was white, with pink
and red hearts above the eyes. He felt silly, but at least the fans
weren't booing.

Mad Dog Markowitz was laughing so hard that the Masked Maverick locked him into a half nelson right away. Mad Dog quickly twisted free, and they got down to some serious wrestling. For several minutes neither man could keep the upper hand. Finally, the Maverick flipped Mad Dog upside down, dropped him onto his head in a perfect piledriver, and then pinned him to the mat.

On the count of three, the Masked Maverick let out a Maverick Victory Yodel so loud that people covered their ears all the way back to the fifth row. Then he covered his own ears to block out the horrible boos and hisses and the unkind names the fans were calling him.

That night, the Maverick refused even to speak to his manager. He went straight home and put on his fanciest red-and-black mask. "If the fans are going to boo me anyway, I am going to wear my favorite mask," he told his cat, Petunia. "But next Saturday will be my last match."

Saturday the Masked Maverick was up against the Brooklyn Bonecrusher. The Bonecrusher was the tallest, the widest, and the meanest wrestler on the whole circuit. He was also the biggest cheater. Besides the usual toe-stomping and nose-twisting, the Bonecrusher loved to pull hair, by the fistful. Worse yet, no one could get him back because the Bonecrusher had less hair than a bowling ball. Some wrestlers said (behind his back, of course) that the Bonecrusher was so ugly that no hair would stay on his head. Beating the Bonecrusher one last time will be the perfect way to end my career, thought the Masked Maverick.

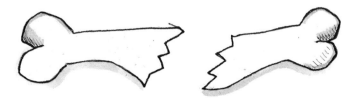

The arena was packed. The Brooklyn Bonecrusher stomped in wearing his trademark necklace of pig knuckle bones. He crunched one between his teeth and spit it at the referee.

The fans screamed and stomped their feet as the wrestlers entered the squared circle.

The Bonecrusher made the first move, turning the handshake into an armwringer before the referee was even out of the way. Then he threw the Masked Maverick into the turnbuckle. As the Maverick wheezed, the Bonecrusher charged. The Masked Maverick dodged at the last minute, skipping into the center of the ring.

The two circled each other for a moment, arms out, then rushed together in a clinch. The Maverick hooked one of the Bonecrusher's arms in a chicken-wing hold, but he couldn't reach the other arm.

The Bonecrusher twisted loose, then caught the Maverick in a head lock. The Bonecrusher smacked the Masked Maverick's head with his free hand, but found no hair to grab. So he hooked the mask at the base of the neck and pulled that instead. The front edge of the mask cut into the Maverick's throat but the Bonecrusher kept pulling. The seams of the mask began to rip, then suddenly the mask came away in the Bonecrusher's hand. In his surprise, he loosened his hold.

The Masked Maverick jumped away. His most favorite, most beautiful, very first mask was nothing but pitiful little black and red shreds, dangling from the Bonecrusher's paw.

The crowd leaped to their feet. In the ring was something they had never seen before: the Masked Maverick's face.

Then they saw something else they had never seen before: the Masked Maverick mad. Really mad. Teeth-gritting, eye-bulging, howling mad. The Bonecrusher took a step back.

Head down and howling, the Masked Maverick charged, knocking the Bonecrusher into the ropes. He grabbed the Bonecrusher's left arm and flipped him over his shoulder, smashing him to the floor. As the Bonecrusher tried to get up, the Maverick hit him with a flying tackle and scrambled onto his back. The Masked Maverick pulled the cheater's legs into the Boston crab pin and the match was over.

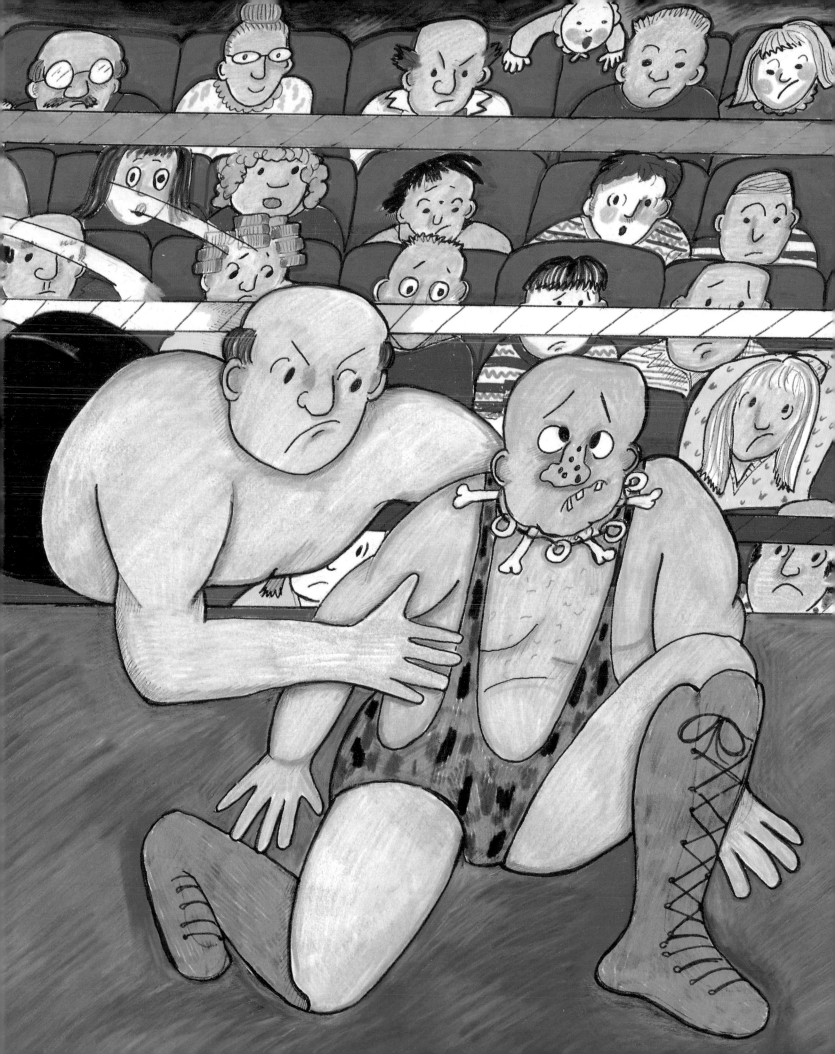

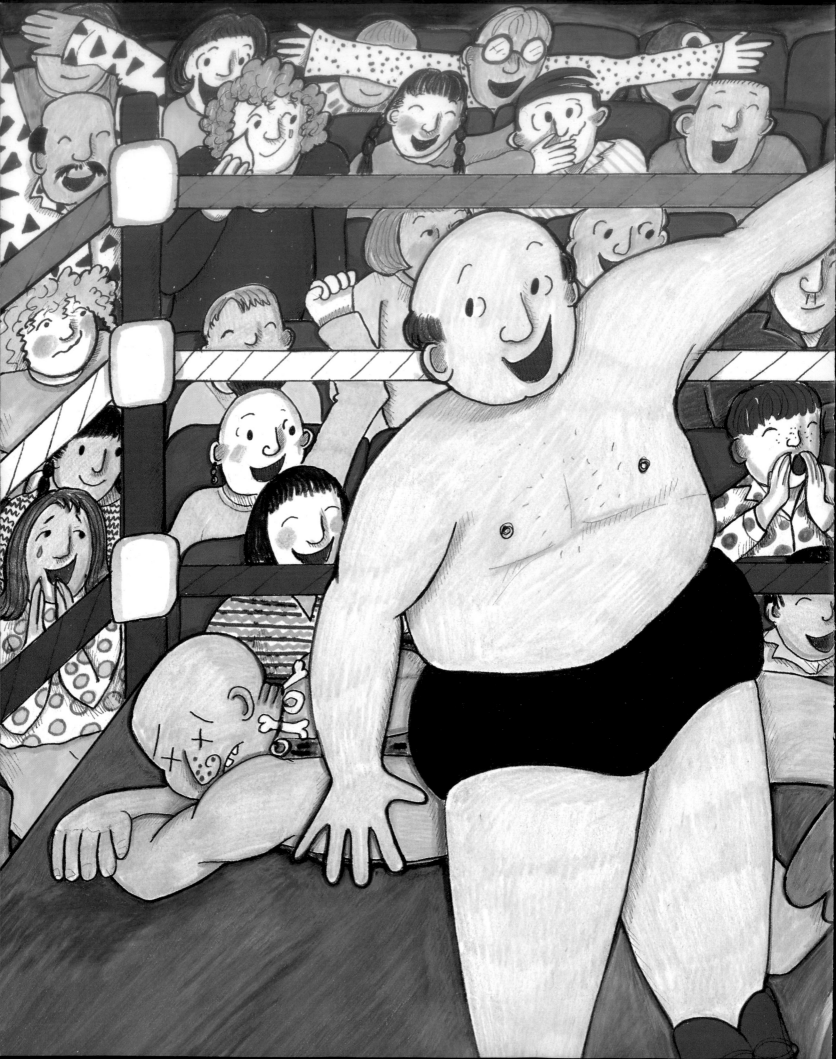

The Masked Maverick threw back his head and let rip his Maverick Victory Yodel. When the referee held up his hand this time, the Masked Maverick heard the sweetest sound in the world. The crowd was hooting and hollering and whistling. They were clapping and crying and CHEERING. For the first time ever, the Masked Maverick's face had been seen in the ring. And the crowd loved it!

From that day on, the Masked Maverick wrestled under a new name: the UnMasked Maverick. And whenever he won, as the referee held up his hand, the crowds cheered and the UnMasked Maverick smiled.